Charles J. Fox

# A Letter From the Right Honourable Charles James Fox

To the worthy and independent electors of the city and liberty of

Westminster. Edition 13

Charles J. Fox

**A Letter From the Right Honourable Charles James Fox**
*To the worthy and independent electors of the city and liberty of Westminster.*
*Edition 13*

ISBN/EAN: 9783337195656

Printed in Europe, USA, Canada, Australia, Japan

Cover: Foto ©Andreas Hilbeck / pixelio.de

More available books at **www.hansebooks.com**

# MR. FOX'S LETTER

TO THE

# ELECTORS OF WESTMINSTER.

---

A

# LETTER

FROM THE

RIGHT HONOURABLE

## CHARLES JAMES FOX,

TO THE

WORTHY AND INDEPENDENT

## ELECTORS

OF THE

## CITY and LIBERTY of WESTMINSTER.

THE THIRTEENTH EDITION

*LONDON:*

PRINTED FOR J. DEBRETT, OPPOSITE BURLINGTON HOUSE,
PICCADILLY.

1793.

A

# L E T T E R, &c.

TO vote in fmall minorities is a mif-
fortune to which I have been fo
much accuftomed, that I cannot be expected
to feel it very acutely.

To be the object of calumny and mifreprefentation gives me uneafinefs, it is true,
but an uneafinefs not wholly unmixed with
pride and fatisfaction, fince the experience
of all ages and countries teaches us that calumny and mifreprefentation are frequently
the moft unequivocal teftimonies of the
zeal, and poffibly the effect, with which he

B againft

againſt whom they are directed has ſerved the public.

But I am informed that I now labour under a misfortune of a far different nature from theſe, and which can excite no other ſenſations than thoſe of concern and humiliation. I am told that *you* in general diſapprove my late conduct, and that, even among thoſe whoſe partiality to me was moſt conſpicuous, there are many who, when I am attacked upon the preſent occaſion, profeſs themſelves neither able nor willing to defend me.

That your unfavourable opinion of me (if in fact you entertain any ſuch) is owing to miſrepreſentation, I can have no doubt. To do away the effects of this miſrepreſentation is the object of this letter, and I know of no mode by which I can accompliſh this

object

object at once fo fairly, and (as I hope) fo
effectually, as by ftating to you the different
motions which I made in the Houfe of
Commons in the firft days of this feffion,
together with the motives and arguments
which induced me to make them.——On
the firft day I moved the Houfe to fubfti-
tute, in place of the Addrefs, the following
Amendment:

" To exprefs to His Majefty our moft
" zealous attachment to the excellent con-
" ftitution of this free country, our fenfe
" of the invaluable bleffings which are de-
" rived from it, and our unfhaken deter-
" mination to maintain and preferve it.·····
" To affure His Majefty, that uniting with
" all His Majefty's faithful fubjects in thofe
" fentiments of loyalty to the Throne, and
" attachment to the Conftitution, we feel in
" common with them the deepeft anxiety

" and

" and concern, when we fee thofe meafures
" adopted by the Executive Government,
" which the law authorizes only in cafes of
" infurrection within this realm.

" That His Majefty's faithful Commons,
" affembled in a manner new and alarming
" to the country, think it their firft duty,
" and will make it their firft bufinefs, to
" inform themfelves of the caufes of this
" meafure, being equally zealous to enforce
" a due obedience to the laws on the one
" hand, and a faithful execution of them
" on the other."

My motive for this meafure was, that
I thought it highly important, both in a
conftitutional and a prudential view, that
the Houfe fhould be thoroughly informed
of the ground of calling out the militia, and

of

of its own meeting, before it proceeded upon other bufinefs.

The Law enables the King, in certain cafes, by the advice of his Privy Council, having previoufly declared the caufe, to call forth the militia—and pofitively enjoins, that, whenever fuch a meafure is taken, Parliament fhall be fummoned immediately.

This law, which provided that we fhould meet, feemed to me to point out to us our duty when met, and to require of us, if not by its letter, yet by a fair interpretation of its fpirit, to make it our firft bufinefs, to examine into the caufes, that had been ftated in the Proclamation as the motives for exercifing an extraordinary power lodged in the Crown for extraordinary occafions; to afcertain whether they were

true

true in fact, and whether, if true, they were of such a nature as to warrant the proceeding that had been grounded on them.

Such a mode of conduct, if right upon general principles, appeared to me peculiarly called for by the circumstances under which we were assembled; and by the ambiguity with which the causes of resorting for the first time to this prerogative were stated and defended.

The insurrections (it was said) at Yarmouth, Shields, and other places, gave Ministers a legal right to act; and the general state of the country, independently of these insurrections, made it expedient for them to avail themselves of this right. In other words, insurrection was the *pretext*, the general state of the country the *cause* of the measure.

fure. Yet infurrection was the motive ftated in the Proclamation ; and the Act of Parliament enjoins the diſclofure, not of the pretext, but of the caufe : fo that it appeared to be doubtful whether even the letter of the law had been obeyed ; but if it had, to this mode of profeſſing one motive and acting upon another, however agreeable to the habits of fome men, I thought it my duty to diffuade the Houfe of Commons from giving any fanction or countenance whatever.

In a prudential view, furely information ought to precede judgment ; and we were bound to know what really was the ftate of the country, before we delivered our opinion of it in the Addrefs. Whenever the Houfe is called upon to declare an opinion of this nature, the weight which ought to belong to fuch a declaration, makes it highly

4                              important

important that it fhould be founded on the moft authentic information, and that it fhould be clear and diftinct. Did the Houfe mean to approve the meafure taken by Adminiftration, upon the ground of the public pretence of infurrections? If fo, they were bound to have before them the facts relative to thofe infurrections, to the production of which no objection could be ftated. Did they mean by their Addrefs to declare that the general fituation of the country was in itfelf a juftification of what had been done? Upon this fuppofition, it appeared to me equally neceffary for them fo to inform themfelves, as to enable them to ftate with precifion to the public the circumftances in this fituation to which they particularly adverted. If they faw reafon to fear impending tumults and infurrections, of which the danger was imminent and preffing, the meafures of His Ma-

jefty's

jefty's Minifters might be well enough adapted to fuch an exigency ; but furely the evidence of fuch a danger was capable of being fubmitted either to the Houfe or to a Secret Committee; and of its exiftence without fuch evidence, no man could think it becoming for fuch a body as the Houfe of Commons to declare their belief.

If therefore the Addrefs was to be founded upon either of the fuppofitions above ftated, a previous enquiry was abfolutely neceffary. But there were fome whofe apprehenfions were directed not fo much to any infurrections, either actually exifting or immediately impending, as to the progrefs of what are called French opinions, propagated (as is fuppofed) with induftry, and encouraged by fuccefs; and to the mifchiefs which might in future time arife from the fpirit of difobedience and diforder, which thefe doctrines are calculated to infpire.

C     This

This danger, they faid, was too notorious to require proof; its reality could better be afcertained by the feparate obfervations of individual members, than by any proceeding which the Houfe could inftitute in its collective capacity; and upon this ground, therefore, the Addrefs might be fafely voted, without any previous enquiry.

To have laid any ground for approving without examination, was a great point gained for thofe who wifhed to applaud the conduct of Adminiftration; but in this inftance I fear the foundation has been laid, without due regard to the nature of the fuperftructure, which it is intended to fupport; for, if the danger confift in falfe but feducing theories, and our apprehenfions be concerning what fuch theories may in procefs of time produce, to fuch an evil it is difficult to conceive how any of the meafures which have been purfued are in any

degree

degree applicable. Opinions muſt have
taken the ſhape of overt acts, before they
can be reſiſted by the fortifications in the
Tower; and the ſudden embodying of the
Militia, and the drawing of the regular
troops to the capital, ſeem to me meaſures
calculated to meet an immediate, not a
diſtant miſchief.

Impreſſed with theſe notions, I could no
more vote upon this laſt vague reaſon, than
upon thoſe of a more definite nature;
ſince, if in one caſe the premiſes wanted
proof, in the other, where proof was ſaid
to be ſuperfluous, the concluſion was not
juſt. If the majority of the Houſe thought
differently from me, and if this laſt ground
of general apprehenſion of future evils (the
only one of all that were ſtated, upon which
it could with any colour of reaſon be pre-
tended that evidence was not both practi-
cable and neceſſary), appeared to them to

juſtify

juftify the meafures of Government; then I fay they ought to have declared explicitly the true meaning of their vote, and either to have difclaimed diftinctly any belief in thofe impending tumults and infurrections, which had filled the minds of fo many thoufands of our fellow fubjects with the moft anxious apprehenfions; or to have commenced an inquiry concerning them, the refult of which would have enabled the Houfe to lay before the public a true and authentic ftate of the nation, to put us upon our guard againft real perils, and to diffipate chimerical alarms.

I am aware that there were fome perfons who thought that to be upon our guard was fo much our firft intereft, in the prefent pofture of affairs, that even to conceal the truth was lefs mifchievous than to diminifh the public terror. They dreaded inquiry, left it fhould produce light; they

felt

felt fo ftrongly the advantage of obfcurity in infpiring terror, that they overlooked its other property of caufing real peril. They were fo alive to the dangers belonging to falfe fecurity, that they were infenfible to thofe arifing from groundlefs alarms.——In this frame of mind they might for a moment forget that integrity and fincerity ought ever to be the characteriftic virtues of a Britifh Houfe of Commons; and while they were compelled to admit that the Houfe could not, without inquiry, profefs its belief of dangers, which (if true) might be fubftantiated by evidence, they might neverthelefs be unwilling that the falutary alarm (for fuch they deemed it) arifing from thefe fuppofed dangers in the minds of the people, fhould be wholly quieted. What they did not themfelves credit, they might wifh to be believed by others. Dangers, which they confidered as diftant,

they

they were not difpleafed that the public
fhould fuppofe near, in order to excite
more vigorous exertions.

To thefe fyftems of crooked policy and
pious fraud I have always entertained a kind of
inftinctive and invincible repugnance; and,
if I had nothing elfe to advance in defence
of my conduct but this feeling, of which I
cannot diveft myfelf, I fhould be far from
fearing your difpleafure. But are there,
in truth, no evils in a falfe alarm, befides
the difgrace attending thofe who are concerned in propagating it? Is it nothing to
deftroy peace, harmony and confidence,
among all ranks of citizens? Is it nothing
to give a general credit and countenance to
fufpicions, which every man may point as
his worft paffions incline him? In fuch a
ftate, all political animofities are inflamed.
We confound the miftaken fpeculatift with
the defperate incendiary. We extend the
prejudices which we have conceived againft
indi-

individuals to the political party or even to the religious fect of which they are members. In this spirit a Judge declared from the bench, in the laft century, that poifoning was a Popifh trick, and I fhould not be furprifed if fome Bifhops were now to preach from the pulpit that fedition is a Prefbyterian or a Unitarian vice. Thofe who differ from us in their ideas of the conftitution, in this paroxyfm of alarm we confider as confederated to deftroy it. Forbearance and toleration have no place in our minds; for who can tolerate opinions, which, according to what the Deluders teach, and rage and fear incline the Deluded to believe, attack our Lives, our Properties, and our Religion?

This fituation I thought it my duty, if poffible, to avert, by promoting an inquiry. By this meafure the guilty, if fuch there are, would have been detected, and the innocent liberated from fufpicion.

My

My propofal was rejected by a great majority. I defer with all due refpect to their
opinion, but retain my own.

My next motion was for the infertion of
the following words into the Addrefs :·····
" Trufting that your Majefty will employ
" every means of negociation, confiftent
" with the honour and fafety of this coun-
" try, to avert the calamities of war."

My motive in this inftance is too obvious
to require explanation ; and I think it the
lefs neceffary to dwell much on this fubject,
becaufe, with refpect to the defirablenefs of
peace at all times, and more particularly in
the prefent, I have reafon to believe that
your fentiments do not differ from mine.
If we looked to the country where the caufe
of war was faid principally to originate, the
fituation of the United Provinces appeared
to me to furnifh abundance of prudential

9                                             argu-

arguments in favour of peace. If we looked to Ireland, I faw nothing there that would not difcourage a wife ftatefman from putting the connection between the two kingdoms to any unneceffary hazard. At home, if it be true that there are feeds of difcontent, War is the hot-bed in which thefe feeds will fooneft vegetate; and of all wars, in this point of view, that war is moft to be dreaded, in the caufe of which Kings may be fuppofed to be more concerned than their fubjects.

I wifhed, therefore, moft earneftly for peace; and experience had taught me, that the voice even of a Minority in the Houfe of Commons, might not be wholly without effect, in deterring the King's Minifters from irrational projects of war. Even upon this occafion, if I had been more fupported, I am perfuaded our chance of preferving the bleffings of peace would be better than it appears to be at prefent.

D

I come

I come now to my third motion,
" That an humble addrefs be prefented
" to his Majefty, that his Majefty will be
" gracioufly pleafed to give directions, that
" a Minifter may be fent to Paris, to treat
" with thofe perfons who exercife provi-
" fionally the functions of executive go-
" vernment in France, touching fuch points
" as may be in difcuffion between his Ma-
" jefty and his Allies, and the French Na-
" tion;" which, if I am rightly informed,
is that which has been moft generally dif-
approved. It was made upon mature con-
fideration, after much deliberation with
myfelf, and much confultation with others ;
and notwithftanding the various mifrepre-
fentations of my motives in making it, and
the mifconceptions of its tendency, which
have prepoffeffed many againft it, I cannot
repent of an act, which, if I had omitted,
I fhould think myfelf deficient in the duty
which

which I owe to you, and to my country at large.

The motives which urged me to make it were, the fame defire of peace which actuated me in the former motion, if it could be preferved on honourable and fafe terms, and if this were impoffible, an anxious wifh that the grounds of war might be juft, clear, and intelligible.

If we or our ally have fuffered injury or infult, or if the independence of Europe be menaced by inordinate and fuccefsful ambition, I know no means of preferving peace but by obtaining reparation for the injury, fatisfaction for the infult, or fecurity againft the defign, which we apprehend; and I know no means of obtaining

any

any of thefe objects but by addreffing ourfelves to the Power of whom we complain.

If the exclufive navigation of the Scheld, or any other right belonging to the States General, has been invaded, the French Executive Council are the invaders, and of them we muft afk redrefs. If the rights of neutral nations have been attacked by the decree of the 19th of November, the National Convention of France have attacked them, and from that Convention, through the organ by which they fpeak to foreign courts and nations, their Minifter for foreign affairs, we muft demand explanation, difavowal, or fuch other fatisfaction as the cafe may require. If the manner in which the fame Convention have received and anfwered fome of our country-

4                                          men,

men, who have addreffed them, be thought
worthy notice, precifely of the fame perfons, and in the fame manner, muft we
demand fatisfaction upon that head alfo. If
the fecurity of Europe, by any conquefts
made or apprehended, be endangered to
fuch a degree, as to warrant us, on the
principles as well of juftice as of policy,
to enforce by arms a reftitution of conquefts
already made, or a renunciation of fuch as
may have been projected, from the Executive Power of France, in this inftance
again, muft we afk fuch reftitution, or fuch
renunciation. How all, or any of thefe
objects could be attained, but by negociation, carried on by authorifed Minifters,
I could not conceive. I knew indeed that
there were fome perfons, whofe notions
of dignity were far different from mine,
and who, in that point of view, would
have preferred a clandeftine, to an avowed

nego-

negociation; but I confeſs I thought this mode of proceeding neither honourable nor ſafe; and, with regard to ſome of our complaints, wholly impracticable.——Not honourable, becauſe, to ſeek private and circuitous channels of communication, ſeems to ſuit the conduct, rather of ſuch as ſue for a favour, than of a great nation, which demands ſatisfaction. Not ſafe, becauſe neither a declaration from an unauthoriſed agent, nor a mere gratuitous repeal of the decrees complained of, (and what more could ſuch a negociation aim at?) would afford us any ſecurity againſt the revival of the claims which we oppoſe; and laſtly, impracticable with reſpect to that part of the queſtion, which regards the ſecurity of Europe, becauſe ſuch ſecurity could not be provided for by the repeal of a decree, or any thing that might be the reſult of a private negociation, but could only be ob-

taincd

tained by a formal treaty, to which the exifting French government muft of necef- fity be a party ; and I know of no means by which it can become a party to fuch a treaty, or to any treaty at all, but by a Mi- nifter publicly authorifed, and publicly re- ceived. Upon thefe grounds, and with thefe views, as a fincere friend to peace, I thought it my duty to fuggeft, what ap- peared to me, on every fuppofition, the moft eligible, and, if certain points were to be infifted upon, the only means of pre- ferving that invaluable blefting.

But I had ftill a further motive ; and if peace could not be preferved, I confidered the meafure which I recommended as highly ufeful in another point of view. To declare war, is, by the Conftitution, the prerogative of the King ; but to grant

or

or with-hold the means of carrying it on, is (by the fame Conftitution) the privilege of the People, through their Reprefentatives; and upon the People at large, by a law paramount to all Conftitutions---the Law of Nature and Neceffity, muft fall the burdens and fufferings, which are the too fure attendants upon that calamity. It feems therefore reafonable that they, who are to pay, and to fuffer, fhould be diftinctly informed of the object for which war is made, and I conceived nothing would tend to this information fo much as an avowed negociation; becaufe from the refult of fuch a negociation, and by no other means, could we, with any degree of certainty, learn, how far the French were willing to fatisfy us in all, or any of the points, which have been publicly held forth as the grounds of complaint againft them.—If in none of

thefe

thefe any fatisfactory explanation were given, we fhould all admit, provided our original grounds of complaint were juft, that the war would be fo too :---if in fome— we fhould know the fpecific fubjects upon which fatisfaction was refufed, and have an opportunity of judging whether or not they were a rational ground of difpute :— if in all—and a rupture were neverthelefs to take place, we fhould know that the public pretences were not the real caufes of the war.

In the laft cafe which I have put, I fhould hope there is too much fpirit in the people of Great Britain, to fubmit to take a part in a proceeding founded on deceit; and in either of the others, whether our caufe were weak or ftrong, we fhould at all events efcape that laft of infamies, the fufpicion of being a party to the Duke of

E                    Brunfwick's

Brunfwick's Manifeftoes *. But this is not all. Having afcertained the precife caufe of war, we fhould learn the true road to peace ; and if the caufe fo afcertained appeared adequate, then wc fhould look for peace through war, by vigorous exertions and liberal fupplies : if inadequate, the Con-

---

* I have heard that the Manifeftoes are not to be confidered as the acts of the Illuftrious Prince whofe name I have mentioned, and that the threats contained in them were never meant to be carried into execution. I hear with great fatisfaction whatever tends to palliate the Manifefloes themfelves ; and with ftill more any thing that tends to difconnect them from the name which is affixed to them, becaufe the great abilities of the perfon in queftion, his extraordinary gallantry, and above all his mild and paternal government of his fubjects, have long fince impreffed me with the higheft refpect for his character ; and upon this account it gave me much concern when I heard that he was engaged in an enterprize, where, according to my ideas, true glory could not be acquired.

ftitution

ſtitution would furniſh us abundance of means, as well through our repreſentatives, as by our undoubted right to petition King and Parliament, of impreſſing his Majeſty's Miniſters with ſentiments ſimilar to our own, and of engaging them to compromiſe, or, if neceſſary, to relinquiſh an object, in which we did not feel intereſt ſufficient to compenſate to us for the calamities and hazard of a war.

To theſe reaſonings it appeared to me, that they only could object with conſiſtency, who would go to war with France on account of her internal concerns; and who would conſider the re-eſtabliſhment of the old, or at leaſt ſome other form of government, as the fair object of the conteſt. Such perſons might reaſonably enough argue, that with thoſe whom they are determined to deſtroy, it is uſeleſs to treat.

To

To arguments of this nature, however, I paid little attention; becaufe the eccentric opinion upon which they are founded was exprefsly difavowed, both in the King's Speech and in the Addreffes of the two Houfes of Parliament: and it was an additional motive with me for making my motion, that, if fairly debated, it might be the occafion of bringing into free difcuffion that opinion, and of feparating more diftinctly thofe who maintained and acted upon it from others, who from different motives (whatever they might be) were difinclined to my propofal.

But if the objections of the violent party appeared to me extravagant, thofe of the more moderate feemed wholly unintelligible. Would they make and continue war, till they can force France to a counter-revolution? No; this they difclaim. What then is to be the termination

mination of the war to which they would excite us? I anfwer confidently, that it can be no other than a negociation, upon the fame principles and with the fame men as that which I recommend. I fay the fame principles, becaufe after war peace cannot be obtained but by a treaty, and a treaty neceffarily implies the independency of the contracting parties. I fay the fame men, becaufe though they *may* be changed before the happy hour of reconciliation arrives, yet that change, upon the principles above ftated, would be merely accidental, and in no wife a neceffary preliminary to peace: for I cannot fuppofe that they who difclaim making war *for* a change, would yet think it right to continue it *till* a change; or, in other words, that the blood and treafure of this country fhould be expended in a hope that—not our efforts—but time and chance may produce a new government in France, with which it would

be

be more agreeable to our Minifters to negociate than with the prefent. And it is further to be obferved, that the neceffity of
fuch a negociation will not in any degree
depend upon the fuccefs of our arms, fince
the reciprocal recognition of the independency of contracting parties is equally neceffary to thofe who exact and to thofe who
offer facrifices for the purpofe of peace.
I forbear to put the cafe of ill fuccefs, becaufe to contemplate the fituation to which
we, and efpecially our ally, might in fuch an
event be placed, is a tafk too painful to be
undertaken but in a cafe of the laft neceffity.
Let us fuppofe therefore the fkill and gallantry of our failors and foldiers to be
crowned with a feries of uninterrupted victories, and thofe victories to lead us to the
legitimate object of a juft war, a fafe and
honourable peace. The terms of fuch a
peace (I am fuppofing that Great Britain

is to dictate them) may confist in satif-
faction, restitution, or even by way of in-
demnity to us or to others, in cession of
territory on the part of France. Now that
fuch satisfaction may be honourable, it muft
be made by an avowed Minifter; that fuch
reftitution or ceffion may be fafe or honourable, they muft be made by an independent
power, competent to make them. And thus
our very fucceffes and victories will neceffarily lead us to that meafure of negociation
and recognition, which, from the diftorted
fhape in which paffion and prejudice repre-
fent objects to the mind of man, has by fome
been confidered as an act of humiliation
and abafement.

I have reafon to believe there are fome
who think my motion unexceptionable
enough in itfelf, but ill-timed. The time
was not in my choice. I had no opportu-

2                                              nity

nity of making it fooner; and, with a view to its operation refpecting peace, I could not delay it. To me, who think that public intercourfe with France, except during actual war, ought always to fubfift, the firft occafion that prefented itfelf, after the interruption of that intercourfe, feemed of courfe the proper moment for preffing its renewal. But let us examine the objections upon this head of Time in detail. They appeared to me to be principally Four——

1ft. That by fending a Minifter to Paris at that period, we fhould give fome countenance to a proceeding*, moft unanimoufly, and

* Since this was written, we have learned the fad cataftrophe of the proceeding to which I alluded. Thofe, however, who feel the force of my argument, will perceive that it is not at all impaired by this revolting act of cruelty and injuftice. Indeed, if I were inclined to fee any connection between the two fubjects, I fhould rather feel additional regret for the rejection

of

and moft juftly reprobated, in every country of Europe.

To this objection I need not, I think, give any other anfwer, than that it refts upon an opinion, that by fending a Minifter we pay fome compliment, implying approbation, to the prince or ftate to whom we fend him ; an opinion which, for the honour of this country, I muft hope to be wholly erroneous. We had a Minifter at Verfailles, when Corfica was bought and enflaved. We had Minifters at the German courts, at the time of the infamous partition of Poland. We have generally a refiden: Conful, who acts as a Minifter to the piratical republic of Algiers ; and we have more than once fent

of a motion which might have afforded one chance more of preventing an act concerning which (out of France) I will venture to affirm that there is not throughout Europe one diffentient voice.

F　　　　　embaffies

embaffies to Emperors of Morocco, reeking from the blood through which, by the murder of their neareft relations, they had waded to their thrones. In none of thefe inftances was any fanction given by Great Britain to the tranfactions by which power had been acquired, or to the manner in which it had been exercifed.

2dly. That a recognition might more properly take place at the end, and as the refult of a private communication, and (in the phrafe ufed upon a former occafion) as the price of peace, than gratuitoufly at the outfet of a negociation.

I cannot help fufpecting, that they who urge this objection have confounded the prefent cafe with the queftion, formerly fo much agitated, of American Independence. In this view they appear to me wholly dif-

fimilar

fimilar—I pray to God that, in all other refpects, they may prove equally fo. To recognize the Thirteen States, was in effect to withdraw a claim of our own, and it might fairly enough be argued that we were entitled to fome price or compenfation for fuch a facrifice. Even upon that occafion, I was of opinion that a gratuitous and preliminary acknowledgment of their independence was moft confonant to the principles of magnanimity and policy; but in this inftance we have no facrifice to make, for we have no claim; and the reafons for which the French muft wifh an avowed and official intercourfe, can be only fuch as apply equally to the mutual intereft of both nations, by affording more effectual means of preventing mifunderftandings, and fecuring peace.

I would further recommend to thofe who

prefs

prefs this objection, to confider whether, if recognition be really a facrifice on our part, the Miniftry have not already made that facrifice by continuing to act upon the commercial treaty as a treaty ftill in force. Every contract muft be at an end when the contracting parties have no longer any exift-ence either in their own perfons or by their reprefentatives. After the tenth of Auguft the political exiftence of Louis XVI. who was the contracting party in the treaty of com-merce, was completely annihilated. The only queftion therefore is, Whether the Execu-tive Council of France did or did not repre-fent the political power fo annihilated. If we fay they did not, the contracting party has no longer any political exiftence either in his perfon or by reprefentation, and the treaty becomes null and void. If we fay they did, then we have actually acknowledged them as reprefentatives, (for the time at leaft) of

what

what was the Executive Government in
France. In this character alone do they
claim to be acknowledged, fince their very
ftyle defcribes them as a Provifional Executive Council and nothing elfe. If we
would preferve our treaty we could not do
lefs; by fending a Minifter we fhould not
do more *.

3dly. That our Ambaffador having been
recalled, and no Britifh Minifter having
refided at Paris, while the conduct of the

---

* If my argument is fatisfactory, I have proved
that we have recognifed the Executive Council; and
it is notorious, that through the medium of Mr.
Chauvelin we have negociated with them. But
although we have both negociated and recognized,
it would be difhonourable, it feems, to negociate in
fuch a manner as to imply recognition. How nice
are the points upon which great bufineffes turn!
how remote from vulgar apprehenfion !

[ French

French was inoffensive with respect to us and our ally, it would be mortifying to send one thither, just at the time when they began to give us cause of complaint.

Mortifying to whom? Not certainly to the House of Commons, who were not a party to the recall of Lord Gower, and who, if my advice were followed, would lose no time in replacing him. To the Ministers possibly *; and if so, it ought to be a warning to the House, that it should not, by acting like the Ministers, lose the proper, that is, the first opportunity, and thereby throw ex-

---

* I do not think it would have been mortifying even to them, because in consequence of the discussions which had arisen, a measure which had been before indifferent might become expedient; but as this point made no part of my consideration, I have not thought it incumbent upon me to argue it.

trinfic difficulties of its own creation in the way of a meafure, in itfelf wife and falutary.

4thly. That by acting in the manner propofed we might give ground of offence to thofe powers, with whom, in cafe of war, it might be prudent to form connection and alliance.

This objection requires examination. Is it meant that our treating with France in its prefent ftate will offend the German Powers, by fhewing them that our ground of quarrel is different from theirs? If this be fo, and if we adhere to the principles which we have publicly ftated, I am afraid we muft either offend or deceive, and in fuch an alternative I truft the option is not difficult.

If it be faid, that, though our original grounds of quarrel were different, yet we
may

may, in return for the aid they may afford
us in obtaining our objects, aſſiſt them in
theirs of a counter-revolution, and enter
into an offenſive alliance for that purpoſe—
I anſwer, that our having previouſly treated
would be no impediment to ſuch a mea-
ſure. But if it were, I freely confeſs that this
conſideration would have no influence with
me ; becauſe ſuch an alliance, for ſuch a
purpoſe, I conceive to be the greateſt calamity that can befall the Britiſh nation : for
let us not attempt to deceive ourſelves; whatever poſſibility or even probability there
may be of a counter-revolution, from internal agitation and diſcord, the means of
producing ſuch an event by external force,
can be no other than the conqueſt of France.
The conqueſt of France !!!—O! calum-
niated cruſaders, how rational and moderate were your objects !—O! much injured
Louis XIV. upon what ſlight grounds have

you

you been accufed of reftlefs and immode-
rate ambition!—O! tame and feeble Cer-
vantes, with what a timid pencil and faint
colours have you painted the portrait of a
difordered imagination!

I have now ftated to you fully, and I truft
fairly, the arguments that perfuaded me to
the courfe of conduct which I have purfued.
In thefe confifts my defence, upon which
you are to pronounce; and I hope I fhall
not be thought prefumptuous, when I fay,
that I expect with confidence a favourable
verdict.

If the reafonings which I have adduced
fail of convincing you, I confefs indeed that
I fhall be difappointed, becaufe to my un-
derftanding they appear to have more of
irrefragable demonftration than can often be
hoped for in political difcuffions; but even

in

in this cafe, if you fee in them probability
fufficient to induce you to believe that,
though not ftrong enough to convince *you*,
they, and not any finifter or oblique motives, did in fact actuate *me*, I have ftill
gained my caufe; for in this fuppofition,
though the propriety of my conduct may
be doubted, the rectitude of my intentions
muft be admitted.

Knowing therefore the juftice and can-
dour of the tribunal to which I have appeal-
ed, I wait your decifion without fear—Your
approbation I anxioufly defire, but your
acquittal I confidently expect.

Pitied for my fuppofed mifconduct by
fome of my friends, openly renounced by
others, attacked and mifreprefented by my
enemies,—to you I have recourfe for refuge
and protection; and confcious, that if I had

6                                    fhrunk

shrunk from my duty, I should have merited your cenfure, I feel myfelf equally certain, that by acting in conformity to the motives which I have explained to you, I can in no degree have forfeited the efteem of the city of Weftminfter, which it has fo long been the firft pride of my life to enjoy, and which it fhall be my conftant endeavour to preferve.

C. J. FOX.

South Street, Jan. 26, 1793.

PARLIAMENTARY REGISTER, 1793.

*This Day are publifhed, price* 1s. *each,*

## NUMBERS V. AND VI. OF THE PRESENT SESSION;

Containing a faithful Report of the Debates and Proceedings in both Houfes of Parliament, REVISED and COLLATED with the NOTES of SEVERAL MEMBERS.

THE PARLIAMENTARY REGISTER: or, The Hiftory of the Proceedings and Debates in both HOUSES of PARLIAMENT; containing an accurate report of the moft interefting fpeeches and motions, authentic copies of all important letters and other papers laid before the Houfe, during the PRESENT SESSION of PARLIAMENT.

*\*\** At the defire of feveral perfons of diftinguifhed abilities and rank, this work was undertaken. The favourable reception it has met with during the three laft and prefent Parliaments, not only demands the moft grateful acknowledgments of the Editors, but encourages them to profecute a continuation of the fame during the prefent Parliament. For this purpofe, and to prevent mifreprefentation, they beg leave again to folicit the affiftance of all their former friends, and every other gentleman.

A ftrict attention will be paid to all commands and favours; nor will any affiduity or care be wanting to preferve that truth and accuracy for which this work has hitherto been diftinguifhed.

The PARLIAMENTARY REGISTER of the FIRST and SECOND SESSIONS of the PRESENT PARLIAMENT; in 6 volumes, 8vo. price 2l. 16s. half bound and lettered.

The PARLIAMENTARY REGISTER, from the General Election in 1780, to the Diffolution of Parliament in 1784, in 14 volumes, 5l. 5s. half bound and lettered.

The PARLIAMENTARY REGISTER, from the General Election in 1784, to the Diffolution of Parliament in 1790, in 13 volumes, price 6l. 12s. half bound and lettered.